Operation Library!

D1016891

Adapted by Tina Gallo
Ready-to-Read

Simon Spotlight
New York London Toronto Sydney New Delhi

SIMON SPOTLIGHT
An imprint of Simon & Schuster Children's Publishing Division
1230 Avenue of the Americas, New York, New York 10020
This Simon Spotlight edition May 2020
DreamWorks The Boss Baby: Back in Business © 2020 DreamWorks Animation LLC.
All Rights Reserved. All rights reserved, including the right of reproduction in whole
or in part in any form.
SIMON SPOTLIGHT, READY-TO-READ, and colophon are registered trademarks of
Simon & Schuster, Inc.
For information about special discounts for bulk purchases, please contact Simon &
Schuster Special Sales at 1-866-506-1949 or business@simonandschuster.com.
Manufactured in the United States of America 0320 LAK
10 9 8 7 6 5 4 3 2 1
ISBN 978-1-5344-6421-6 (hc)
ISBN 978-1-5344-6420-9 (pbk)
ISBN 978-1-5344-6422-3 (eBook)

Today, Boss Baby was going to the library with his grandmother and his brother, Tim.

Grandma brought

Boss Baby

over to story time.

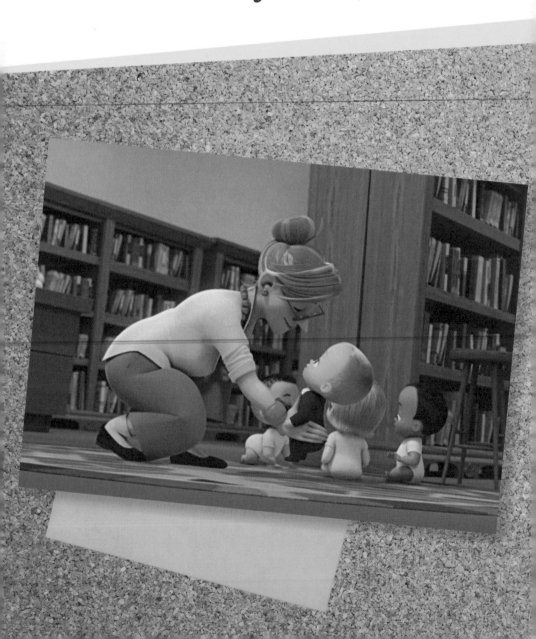

Tim was going
to read comic books.

Boss Baby heard

someone call his name.

It was Staci, his friend from Baby Corp.

Staci loved story time!
It was her favorite time
of day.

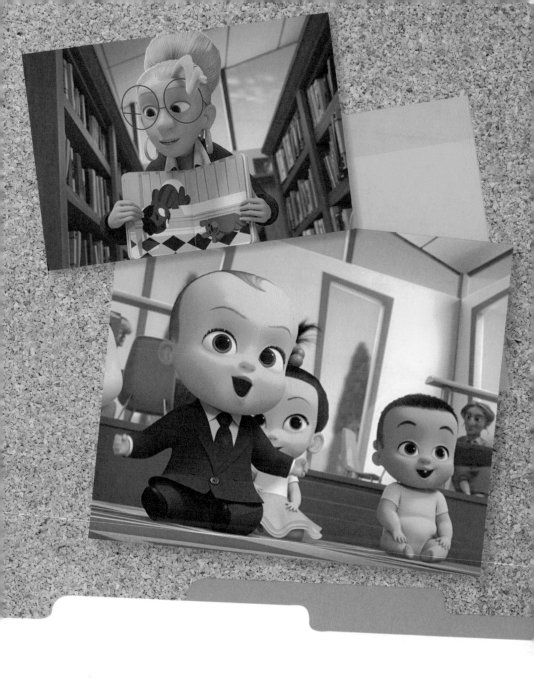

Boss Baby really liked
story time too!

"Story time
again tomorrow?"
his grandma asked.

Boss Baby

could not wait!

The next day,
Boss Baby went back
to the library.

But even though the babies loved story time, not everyone at the library did.

"A library is supposed to be quiet," someone said. It was Frederick Estes, an enemy of Baby Corp.

"Babies do not
belong here,"
he said.

The storyteller asked
the babies to be quiet.
But some babies
could not help laughing
at the story.

Boss Baby, Staci, and Jimbo tried not to laugh. But the babies were not quiet enough.

Frederick made
the library end story time!
Tim asked his grandma
to have story time at home.

She told stories about
when she was a young girl.
She would always
stand up for what
she believed in!

The babies decided to take back story time!

The plan was to
scare the grown-ups so
they would make noise.

If the grown-ups were noisy, they would have to leave the library.

The babies scared
the grown-ups.
They were yelling!

Soon, Frederick was the only grown-up in the library.

He heard a noise.

He saw Boss Baby

and Staci.

They scared him!

The plan worked!

"Nice work,"

Boss Baby said.

Story time was saved!

All the babies
were happy.

But the happiest baby
of all . . .

. . . was Staci!